ROYAL ENCHANTMENT

The Skeleton Key series

By

LIA DAVIS

Royal Enchantment
Skeleton Key Series
By: Lia Davis

Published by After Glows
© 2016 Lia Davis

ISBN: 978-1-944060-11-4

Cover Art by JM Rising Horse Designs

www.AuthorLiaDavis.com

Dedication

To my own King, who after 16 years still enchantments me.
Love you with all my heart.

CHAPTER 1

There it is.

A thrill skittered up Ava's spine as she parked her Audi in the gravel driveway of a Victorian tucked in the foothills of the Blue Ridge Mountains. Beautiful didn't seem like the right word to even begin to describe it. Three stories of grey stone with green moss growing up one side loomed over her.

Emerging from her car, she gathered her purse and pulled out the keys to the home. While the outside looked decent enough, she feared the inside needed a lot of work. After all, it'd been empty for almost a decade. But it was the gamble she took when buying the place without doing a walk-through, which her business partner had said she was crazy for doing.

She did, however, ask the seller why it'd been empty for so long. All they said was that the family simply didn't want to deal with it.

Ava didn't know what *it* was, nor did she care. She'd bought the house to flip. And that was what she was going to do. She just hoped she hadn't bitten off more than she could chew.

She tested each porch step before putting her weight on them. *Hmm, pretty sturdy.* Once inside, she scanned the foyer that was bigger than her one-bedroom apartment. Dark, hardwood floors stretched on to a staircase wide enough for four people to walk up side by side. About halfway to the second level, the stairs split into two different sets of steps, each leading to opposite sides of the house.

Glancing up, she gasped at the elegant and very large crystal chandelier. Man, she wished the electricity was already on. She could only imagine how beautiful it was illuminating the entryway.

Jeff, her business partner, had said she was crazy for wasting money on the place. But she couldn't pass it by. It was weird, but she got the feeling that she needed to buy the house, almost like it called out to her. So she'd purchased it with her own money. Sight unseen. Thanks to the inheritance from her parents.

She climbed the stairs and admired the hand-carved rose vine wrapping around the wood rails. Beautiful and detailed. Quickening her steps, she made it to the top of the north wing in record time. Excitement stirred up the butterflies in her belly at what secrets the house might hold. And there were secrets. All old houses had them.

Each room she passed had the same layout, but they were each unique in their design. Color-coded from the walls, to the carpet, drapes, and bedding. *Wow. Had it been a B&B?*

She came to a closed door at the end of the hallway. It was smaller than the other doors, and oddly placed, like it could be a closet. When she tried to open it, she found it was locked. Studying the handle, she noticed that it was the type that took a skeleton key. There weren't many of those locks these days, and she hadn't met one she couldn't break in to.

Ava pulled a hairpin from her bun. She'd picked locks like this one in her grandmother's old house all the time when her cousins had tried to keep her out of their rooms.

It was all in the wrist... The lock didn't release. Hmm. She tried again with no luck.

Damn. She stepped back and scanned the door. The hinges were on the inside. *Odd.*

Just then, her cell rang. Turning from the door, she pulled the smartphone out and answered. "Ava Green speaking."

Kathy, her office assistant, hesitated for a moment before speaking. "Jeff fired me."

"What! He can't do that."

"That's what I said when he called me to tell me not to bother coming in." Kathy released a heavy sigh. "I thought he was joking or mad at you for buying that house. So I went into the office."

Dread slammed into Ava's gut, burning a trail of cold fear through her. "What happened?"

"The place was cleaned out. Furniture, computers, clients' files..."

Ava leaned against the wall and slid to the floor. She and Jeff had been friends for as long as she could remember, and business partners for five years. Sure, he had been having issues with his marriage. But the separation had gone pretty smoothly. Well, as far as Ava knew, anyway. It didn't make sense for him to screw her over. *She* wasn't divorcing him!

"Maybe he found a new office and wanted to surprise me."

A grunt from Kathy soured Ava's mood further. "You are a very smart woman. I know you don't believe that."

"I don't understand why he'd do something like this." Ava searched her memories for signs she may have missed that would have told her this was coming. She'd dismissed his behavior change, blaming it on his separation and pending divorce. Not once had he come into the office smelling of alcohol. Could he have been using drugs? Wouldn't she have known?

Then she remembered the argument they'd had over buying the Victorian she currently sat in. He'd told her they didn't have the funds in the Line of Credit for it. At the time, she thought he was just being difficult because he wasn't getting what he wanted.

"Ava?"

"I'm here." Ava stood and moved to the stairs. She'd left her computer in the car in all the excitement of seeing the inside of the house. "I hope Jeff didn't screw me royally, because I don't have the money to start up another company."

Fucking jerk was going to pay. She'd have to go back to working for a larger realty company until she saved up enough funds to start over.

"I know. I'm just lucky that Frank has a secure job and is able to support both of us." Kathy sighed again. Or was it a sob? Ava's chest tightened.

"I'm so sorry."

"Don't be. None of this is your fault. I'll be in touch." Kathy hung up.

Ava descended the stairs with a heavy heart. She punched in Jeff's number and waited. A recording came on saying the number was no longer in service. Figures. Deep down, she *knew* Jeff had screwed her and skipped town. She couldn't explain it. Her intuition had always been spot on. This time, the knowing was too strong. It also told her that there was something much larger going on.

Her phone rang again. Well, wasn't she the popular one? "Hello."

"Ava?" A female voice on the edge of tears stilled her as she stepped off the last stair.

"Alice, are you okay?"

Alice was Jeff's soon-to-be ex-wife. Even though they weren't close friends, they still talked on occasion, mostly about Jeff being a jerk. Alice sniffed once before answering Ava's question. "Jeff...had an accident."

Oh, dear God. Ava sank down to sit on the bottom step. "Is he...?"

"He's dead." Alice broke into sobs.

Ava squeezed the phone to her ear, not believing that her friend was dead. "What happened?"

After several long moments, the other woman answered. "He was shot."

"Wait. You said he had an accident."

Another sniff, then her soft reply. "Yes. I mean... He was shot which caused the wreck."

Apparently, Alice was confused and in shock. As was Ava. But there were too many questions whirling in her mind, and they kept the grief at bay. Then again, she hadn't been married to the man for fifteen plus years. "Are you alone? You should be with family."

"I'm with my mom and sisters."

"Good." Another ache shot through Ava's chest. The one thing she both loved and hated about her life was that she didn't have any living family. No one to mourn her if she disappeared or died. No one to fight with or to love. In fact, she'd made it her mission to not get attached to people. She could pick up everything and move on at a moment's notice.

Something her parents had done every couple of years. It just seemed natural to her to move. That was another reason she'd bought the house for no good reason.

However, her life was lonely and sad at times.

"Alice, if you need anything, just call me."

There was a softer whisper of a "Thank you" before the line went silent. Tears filled Ava's eyes. Her earlier anger was whisked away, replaced with a sadness she knew too well. Jeff was gone. How? Why?

Opening the local news app on her phone, Eva scrolled to see if there was anything on Jeff's shooting. After about five minutes of scrolling and searching, she found it. The police said it was a possible drive-by.

Man, of all the dumb luck. She logged into her bank app and her password didn't work. After trying two more times, she gave up and called the branch. When the rep answered, Ava gave him all her information. The rep said, "I'm sorry, ma'am, but that account has been closed."

"Closed? When?"

"A few minutes ago."

Ava frowned. How does a dead guy close an account? Or did he? "Who closed it?"

"Alice Moore."

"Thank you." Ava hung up the phone and squeezed it. The business was in Jeff's name, and there was no official agreement between him and Ava. A mistake she was currently paying for. All Alice had to do was show the death certificate to close the account. But even that thought didn't hold much water with Ava. Something weird was going on.

Ava let out a frustrated growl. *Damnit.* Why was she so naive and stupid?

"Why can't I just be swallowed by the earth or something?" Rising to her feet, she climbed back up the stairs, and before she realized it, she was standing outside the locked door again. It bothered her that she couldn't get in. But it was just like her to obsess over something like that. Besides, it didn't make any sense why the door was locked.

She turned and sighed. She really had other things to worry about. One of them was moving her things to the house. It seemed she was out of a job, and had depleated a large chunk of her savings buying the house outright instead of taking a mortgage on it.

You're in deep now. Might as well push ahead and make the best out of the crap situation. Damn Jeff. She'd trusted him.

When she reached the stairs, she spotted something on the floor, a reflection of light like a prism. She bent down to take a closer look and discovered a glass skeleton key sticking out from behind the railing post. It was about four inches long and made of thick glass with a skull on the top. The bottom key portion looked like...well, human teeth.

She picked it up and tested the weight. A couple of ounces, she guessed. Studying it for several moments, she wondered where it had come from. Her thoughts turned to the locked door. No. That would be too easy. However, it *was* a skeleton key. Literally in this case.

What did she have to lose? Pivoting on her heels, she walked to the door, glad no one was around to witness her state of crazy.

She took a deep breath and stuck the key into the lock. Turned. A click sounded a moment before the door swung open. A smile lifted her lips, but it was short-lived as she stared out into a forest. *What-the-ever-loving-freaking-hell*?

Instantly, she closed the door. Surely she was seeing things and needed to call a shrink. Hell, maybe just go to the nearest liquor store.

Okay, Ava. You're not crazy. You may be a little weird at times, but you are not crazy.

She opened the door again and let it swing wide. *Holy crap*. There really was a forest in one of her upstairs rooms. Well, she had asked for the earth to swallow her. She laughed at her attempt at a joke and stepped through the door.

Once she crossed the threshold, the door vanished behind her. Whirling around, she scanned her surroundings. Nothing but trees, bushes, and a whole lot of nature. The house was gone. Everything was so green and full of life, almost magickal.

I'm definitely not in Georgia anymore.

A howl like she'd never heard before cut through the trees in the distance, followed by shouts. Then the sound of horses' hooves pounding the earth grew closer. Her heart jerked to life, beating rapidly as the howls and gallops got louder, nearer, moving in on her too fast.

Desperate to find a hiding spot or at least get out of whatever it was's path, she darted to her right. She hurtled over fallen trees and barreled through the brush. But the howls and shouts still closed in. She cut left, only to realize she'd made a mistake. Thick, thorned bushes stood about six feet tall between two large oaks. *Damn.*

She turned to dart back the way she'd come, only to come nose to nose with a large, snarling animal that appeared half-sabretooth tiger and half-dragon. Large, purple wings stuck out of the beast's back. Its snout was long and dragon-like, with fangs about as big as her hand from tip of middle finger to wrist.

She was trapped like a rabbit on a fox hunt. She just *had* to know what was behind that damn door.

"Charles. Heel." The deep boom of a command came from behind the animal and sent a chill up Ava's spine.

Charles backed off but only enough for the man to step into her line of sight. Ava's heart skipped a few beats as she stared at him. Long, black hair that appeared green in the sunlight cascaded over his shoulders, framing a beautiful yet masculine face. Heat rolled within her abdomen, spreading to the rest of her body. Desire filled her mind, dizzying. The urge to touch him was strong, almost too strong for her to ignore.

What the fuck was wrong with her?

"Who are you?" The man loomed over her, arms folded, revealing the most unusual markings tattooed on his forearms. His words shocked her out of the haze.

Glaring at him, she mimicked his crossed-arm stance and asked her own question. "Where am I?"

He narrowed his gaze on her, but she swore there was a hint of a smile on his lips. Like he approved of her attempt to be brave. "Answer my question first."

Even though it was a command, he spoke the words softer than his previous ones. Still, it wouldn't hurt him to say 'please.' She released a sigh and figured she'd play nice. After all, she had a feeling she was in his world now. "Ava Green. I unlocked a door with a glass skeleton key and ended up here."

He raised a brow and studied her for a moment. "You are from the human realm?"

Umm, yeah, the last time she checked... "And you're not?"

One corner of his mouth twitched. He relaxed his stance and gripped her wrist. "Come with me."

"Where?" Her heart pounded while her mind screamed that she was going to die.

"My home, where I can keep you safe from my enemies."

What the hell did that mean? She planted her feet in place and jerked her arm free, which was easier than she'd expected. "I don't know who you are, and I'm not going anywhere with you."

He stared at her as if he weren't used to being told no. A mix of shock and annoyance became etched onto his face. After a few moments, he reached for her again, but she darted out of the way. He muttered something that wasn't English before saying, "I am Finn, King of the Morna, the Dark Elves."

King? Dark Elves? Okay, she must have hit her head and this was all a dream. Any moment, she'd wake up. Or it could be that Finn was the delusional one. "You do know that elves aren't real, right?"

His brows dipped as he stepped closer to her and waved a hand in front of her face. "Forgive me."

Before she had a chance to question him, everything around her grew dim. Her body went limp in Finn's arms. "What...?"

"Shh. Just sleep."

Sleep sounded wonderful. She closed her eyes and snuggled into his chest as he scooped her up.

CHAPTER 2

"This is a mistake."

Finn glared at his head of security as the male went on about how he was endangering his life. Blah, blah, blah. If Finn went to the bathroom alone, he was endangering his life. "What would you have me do with her?"

A low growl rumbled from the male. "You could have put her in one of the holding cells until I verify who she is."

Fury rushed through him. With his inhuman speed, he was in Kellam's face with his hand around the male's throat. "She will not be locked up like an animal."

Kellam narrowed his crimson eyes and worked his jaw before asking, "What are you not saying?"

"You saw her. She's the one. She's the daughter of Jander and Faylan." Finn backed off and turned toward the bed where he'd placed the female after arriving moments ago. She wasn't just the prophesied female that would set things right again, she was also his mate.

A half-grunt, half-growl escaped Kellam. "So you endanger everyone in the palace by bringing her here?"

"She is under my protection, as much as all my people." Finn didn't want to discuss it anymore. "Your job is to tighten security around the palace and keep her identity a secret. *And* to find out where my uncle is hiding."

Another complication in his life. Quinn, his uncle, had been responsible for starting the plague that had wiped out sixty percent of the population of Edra. Finn suspected he also had something to do with the depleted magick.

Quinn had become predictable in making his threats to claim the throne over the years. However, a few months ago, the messages stopped. That had both Finn and Kellam concerned. Kellam more so than Finn. After all, the palace had a ward around it so no one—who didn't belong—could enter the gates.

"She could have been sent by the rebels." Kellam glared at her suspiciously.

Finn shook his head. "No." It was all the explanation he'd give Kellam. He didn't see what Finn saw apparently. If he did, he wasn't saying so just so he could argue with Finn.

Kellam had been with Finn since his training had started at the age of five. The male knew better than anyone that Finn was stubborn to the core. Once his mind was set, nothing would stop him. Not his uncle. And not the rebels.

Studying the sleeping female, Finn refrained from going to her, releasing her blonde hair from the bun, and threading his fingers through it. From the moment they'd made eye contact in the woods, he'd known who she was. He'd filled with hope that the seer had been right about the prophecy of their savior. Although when the urge to touch her, to claim her as his bride rose up within him, he'd known she was so much more. Precious. The fire in her eyes before he'd put her to sleep told him that she wasn't afraid to take chances, and would do anything to protect herself. Even if she didn't realize her destiny.

"She has no idea who she is." Kellam turned back to Finn, annoyance still weighing heavily in his stare.

Flicking his gaze to Kellam, Finn let out a warning growl to let the male know the conversation was over. When he glanced back at her, Finn meet her blue eyes and his heart skipped several beats. She was his mate, and he'd do anything to make her his bride.

Ava opened her eyes and blinked several times, trying to clear the fog from her brain. Confusion weighed on her like a wet blanket. By walking through that door, she must have entered a portal of some kind. But to where?

Whispered voices from across the room cut into her thoughts. Finn was in some kind of tense conversation with a much larger man. Sitting up in bed, she watched them, noting how...not human the larger man was. He was the tallest person she'd ever seen, towering over Finn by at least four feet or so. But that wasn't the strangest thing about him. His skin was a dark navy blue that appeared black in the shadows. White hair was braided down his back, the tip of the plait brushing the waist of his black pants.

Without looking at her, he snarled at Finn. "She has no idea who she is."

She fisted her hands while meeting Finn's stare. Annoyance raced in her blood. "I know who I am. Who are you?" After flinging the covers off, she marched to the tall blue guy. Before she could get close, Finn appeared in front of her. Yes. Appeared. As if by magick or something. She focused on Finn, then folded her arms. Something in the way he stood protectively between her and the blue guy told her that they were hiding information. "What is going on?"

Finn held out his hand. She didn't take it, so he dropped it. "I sense a power within you. A mixture of both Dark and Light magicks."

He was insane. Had to be. She'd stepped into a world of crazies. "I don't have, nor have I ever had any magick."

Finn nodded. "I can see how this could be very strange to you. Even unbelievable. If you give me a chance, I'd like to explain."

When he lifted his hand this time, she took it after a few moments of hesitation. She hadn't a clue what he was talking about, but she needed to know where she was and how she could get back home. Before the insanity wore off on her.

Her belly chose that moment to rumble, embarrassing her. Finn smiled and tugged her toward the door. "I will feed you."

Food sounded great. Besides, Finn was easy on the eyes. Glancing at him, she caught a glimpse of his pointed ears from under his hair. She jerked to a stop and brushed his hair aside. Before she could touch him, he gripped her wrist and shook his head. "The ears are sensitive."

"You're an elf." The words tumbled out before she'd thought better of it, or realized how crazy it sounded. Sure he'd told her in the forest that he was the King of the Dark Elves, but she really didn't believe him. Elves were myths, weren't they?

One corner of his mouth lifted in a sensual half-smile. "I told you I was. I don't lie. It's a waste of time and air." He leaned in closer so their lips were inches apart. "Besides, I could never lie to you."

"Why?" she breathed out, her heart pounding wildly in her chest, pulsing in her throat.

He frowned and stepped back. "I will explain in private after you eat."

"You can explain *while* I eat." She tugged her hand free from his and crossed her arms.

He narrowed his emerald green eyes, and after a moment, he said, "Very well." Nodding to the other man, Finn gave a tart command, as if annoyed. "Set a meeting with Willow."

Mr. Blue Man let out a soft growl that Ava couldn't help but think was directed at her, then left them alone. She followed Finn when he exited the room. "Who was that?"

"Kellam. He's my head of security."

Okay. "What is he?"

Finn didn't answer right away, just continued to walk down the hall. Fine, she'd save her questions. For a little while anyway. But she would get answers. One way or another.

A moment later, they came to a small reading room. Or at least it looked like one with a floor-to-ceiling bookcase taking up one of the walls. A large bay window was the centerpiece of the room. Instantly, she went to it, knelt on her knees on the bench seat, and peered out. Below was the largest and most beautiful rose garden she'd ever seen. Upon further inspection, she noticed several paths weaving through the garden like a maze. "Beautiful."

"Roses were my mother's favorite flower. She spent hours of every day tending to the garden." Finn sat on the seat next to her, staring out the window. Sorrow rolled from him and reached out to her.

"What happened?"

He lifted his gaze, and her heart broke at the unshed tears; yet, she didn't comment and let him speak when he was ready. After a moment, he looked back out the window. "The Morna and Calim—the Light Elves— went to war a few decades ago. The war threw the balance of our world off. The more unbalanced our world became, the more magick they used."

She sensed that something much darker had happened. "Are you still at war?"

"No. The Light Queen and I formed an enchanted contract." He straightened and lifted his chin. "It's unfortunate that it took a plague that my uncle started to make our parents see what they'd done. My parents, as well as many others, died in that plague."

Reacting on instinct, she covered his hand with hers and said, "Your uncle created a plague?"

"Yes. He started up a group of rebels who were for neither side and claimed to be against the war." Finn worked his jaw, making the muscles in his face flex. "He only wanted to claim the throne and wipe out the Light Elves."

He turned his palm up and closed his hand around hers. Warm, electrifying energy sparked between their palms. When she glanced down, she could see their auras. Something her mother had taught her to do at a young age when she'd started suffering from social anxiety. All she had to do was make sure she was grounded and centered every morning through meditation. And keep her aura a color of blue that wasn't too light or too dark. The color of peacefulness and truth.

In that moment, with hers and Finn's hands joined, there were three colors: dark green, dark blue, and light blue. She knew the green was his, because it made sense to her. The comfortable and healthy color of nature. His hair had a green hue to it—as did his skin, she realized, being as close to him as she was then. However, her aura had never taken both colors of blue at the same time before. "I've never seen it do that before."

"You can see our energies?"

"Yes. Mine is always a medium blue. I have to make sure of it."

He faced her, linking their fingers together as he did. "Why?"

She really didn't want to talk about it with him. After all, they'd just met. And he hadn't really told her where she was. After tugging her hand free, she stood and drifted around the room. "You promised me food and an explanation of where I am."

She caught the slight smirk on his lips before he stood and stalked toward her. "Food is on its way. You are in Edra, the Realm of the Elves."

"How did I get here?"

"You said you had a key and it unlocked a door. My guess is that the door was a portal." He stopped inches from her. "We have been waiting for you."

Waiting for me? "Me? Why?"

With a narrowed gaze, he studied her for a moment. "You don't know?"

"Know what?" She fisted her hands. He wasn't making sense. Why wouldn't he just tell her already?

Just then, a light knock sounded on the door. Finn didn't move from his spot in front of her. "Come in."

The door opened, and a young, petite girl entered carrying a tray. She had purple hair and mocha-colored skin. She met Ava's stare briefly before glancing to Finn and then the floor as she made her way to the table to the left of the bay window. After setting out the plates and pouring what Ava assumed was tea, the girl turned to Finn. "Will there be anything else?"

"No, Fern. Thank you."

She curtsied and left the room.

"Have a seat."

Although Finn's words were soft, she sensed the command in them like a power only he possessed. Maybe so. He was the King, after all.

After taking her seat, she inhaled the savory aromas of thinly sliced steak over steamed vegetables. Her stomach growled. There went pretending she wasn't hungry to get more information from him. Still, she studied him as he took the seat across from her with fluid grace. He was beautiful, yet masculine at the same time.

"Please, eat." He frowned as if uncertain about something. Before she could ask what about, he spoke again. "There is a legend of two elves, one Dark and one Light, who fell in love. Because the union was forbidden, they left Edra to live in the human realm. Their escape sparked a war between my people and the Light ones."

A war? Because two people fell in love? "Why?"

"The male was the Prince of the Calim. He was the only son to the King and Queen."

"But war?"

Finn cut his steak as he continued. "The Calim King demanded my parents' firstborn as payment for losing his only son. Of course, my father refused, so the Light King declared war, blaming the Morna for corrupting his son and people."

He paused to take a bite and chew. Ava pushed her broccoli around her plate, taking in the information. The thought that this whole thing could be a dream drifted through her mind. She didn't understand why he'd told her about the couple and the war. It didn't answer any of her questions.

"The war went on for decades, and used up a lot of the natural magick. We grew weak, both the Calim and Morna. Our ability to self-heal and remain ageless decreased to almost nothing. Then the plague fell upon us, killing most of our people, my parents included." Finn set his fork on the table and rose to stand in front of the window.

Her heart broke for him, even though she could sense a wall go up around his. He most likely hid behind that barrier. She felt the need to comfort him. Instead of reaching out to him, she shared her own loss. "I lost my parents a few years ago. My dad fell ill. Doctors said it was pneumonia and that he was too old to fight it off. Well, they didn't say that exactly, but I got the message. Anyway, a few months after Dad died, Mom passed away. It was as if her mourning sent her into a deep depression and she willed herself to die. She didn't love me enough to stay."

Finn was at her side in a flash. Ava didn't even see the man move. Kneeling at her side, he took her hands in his. When she peered into his dark green eyes, she saw the first signs of tears. "That is not true. When elves mate, it's for life. One dies, the other will follow into the next life."

Confusion rolled through her mind like storm clouds. "Elves? My parents were human."

His eyes sparked like an inner light had been flipped on behind his pupils. After a moment, he drew his brows together. "After Willow, the Queen of the Calim, and I ended the war, a seer prophesied that the child of the lovers would return to us and restore the magick of the land."

"And you think I'm that child?"

A sensual smile lifted one side of his mouth. "You are no child. But yes, you are the one who will forever link the Morna and Calim and restore the magick to Edra."

She tugged her hands free and shook her head. He'd told her the story because he believed the lovers were her parents. That made her half Morna and half Calim. Still, she wasn't sold. "If I am this hybrid elf, why don't I have any powers?"

"Our magicks are limited in the human realm."

He seemed to have an answer for everything. "My parents never had any either, and they didn't have a reason to lie to me my whole life." Anger fueled the pain of loss that surfaced when she first mentioned the two people that had meant the most to her. She pushed her plate to the center of the table and stood. "Thank you for the food, but I need to get home."

By the time she reached the door, Finn was there, blocking her exit. "I can't allow you to leave." He raised one hand and caressed her cheek with his knuckles. "Not yet."

With pursed lips, she stepped back and stared at him, seeing his energy flow around him. *Just because he believes what he said doesn't mean it's the truth.* She crossed her arms. "So you have the power to control my free will?"

A frown formed on his perfect, handsome face. "I do not." The muscle in his temple twitched as if he ground his teeth. "I ask you to stay. With me. We can get to know each other, and you can learn about our realm."

She didn't fail to notice that he referred to Edra as if it were her world instead of just his. "Why? I didn't ask to be here. I was comfortable in my life where I was." With the expectation of the most recent events, that was.

He opened his mouth, then closed it again. A moment later, he broke the eye contact and threaded his fingers through his long, dark hair. "I believe you are who I said you are, and I'd like a chance to show you the truth. Besides, if I am right, then you are in great danger."

"Danger?"

With a short nod, he held out his hand. "Even though Queen Willow and I are bound to a peace treaty, the rebels will kill you to keep you from uniting the two kingdoms."

There it was. The ripple in his aura. He didn't lie to her, but he didn't tell her the whole truth either. However, she'd play long. For now. "Wouldn't I be safe in my own world?"

"No. Not now that you are here. Your presence in the forest would have alerted our enemies. They will be searching for you."

Hmm. "And I'm safe here?"

Emerald eyes locked with hers. "Yes, but only inside the palace walls. I have the palace warded to protect those within, including you."

Again with a half-truth. She had to get out of there. Finn didn't make sense. Hell, none of the crap that had happened in the last hour made sense. "You still haven't answered my question as to why I should stay."

"Your life is in danger now."

She glared at him. She trusted people too much in her life. That's why things like the partnership with Jeff ended with her being shitted on. She simply didn't understand how people could be so hurtful. "You are withholding information from me. Why should I believe anything you say?"

When he opened his mouth to speak, she held up a hand. "Don't tell me another half-truth."

He dropped his shoulders. "I know from the bottom of my soul that you are the hybrid elf we've been waiting for. I also know you are to be my bride."

Her heart stopped for a brief moment, then resumed beating at an alarming rate. His bride? Oh. No. That wasn't happening.

She rushed to the door and ran down the hallway, desperate to find a way out of the palace. Away from Finn.

CHAPTER 3

Ava made it to the edge of the forest before Finn flashed in front of her. Skidding to a halt, she glared at him. Magick rippled around him, darkening his aura. A mix of anger and fear flowed from him and touched her awareness. He truly was afraid for her life.

She flicked her gaze to the large bodyguard behind Finn. Kellam stood with his arms folded like a wall. No, he was more like a dragon, waiting for danger to strike. Turning her attention back to Finn, she pointed at him. "I'm not marrying you. One, I don't know you, and two, I will not marry anyone I'm not in love with."

Finn closed the gap between them, took her hand, and then flattened her palm against his chest. Heat enveloped her, making it impossible to concentrate. His voice was calm and soft when he spoke. "I wouldn't have it any other way. Please stay with me. Learn about my people, our people, and give me a chance to woo you."

A tiny voice in her head screamed to run, but it was her heart that she trusted the most. Even when it led her down a darker path. Maybe she was here for a reason? However, she still wasn't sold on Finn's story of her parents being elves. "I'll give you a day."

A sexy smile lifted the corners of his lips. "That's hardly fair. Give me a month."

A month? Thoughts of home churned in her mind. She had no one waiting on her. In fact, she wasn't sure there was anyone who would miss her. Really, she didn't have anything to lose. Or gain. Sadness settled into her heart. Her life was a lonely, pathetic mess. "One week."

He looped an arm around her waist and meshed their bodies together. Desire rushed through her, making her lightheaded. She took a deep breath to try to clear her thoughts, but his clean, earthy scent only made her want him more. Then he let out a low growl-like sound that vibrated his chest. "Two weeks."

Oh, dear God. "No more."

"Deal."

The sound of that one word made her suddenly think she had just sealed her fate with the devil himself.

She opened her mouth to speak, but Finn placed a finger over her lips in a silent command. A moment later, he moved to stand with his back against her front in a protective stance. Kellam moved in beside Finn then stepped forward. Fear burned her insides as a dark energy touched her psyche. Peeking around him, she couldn't see any signs of a threat, but it was there, lurking.

"What is it?" she whispered.

Finn reached back with one hand and gently squeezed her elbow. "Go inside."

"What is it?" she asked again, a little louder.

Just then, a man…no, an *elf* stepped out of the shadows as if appearing from the darkness. He was about a foot taller than Finn with long, black hair that blended with his tunic and leather pants. His dark gaze met hers, just as a creepy smirk tugged at his mouth. Suddenly, the fear in her gut morphed into a need to protect herself as well as Finn.

Before she could form words to question Finn again, the man spoke. "She has returned, but she is weak."

Kellam let out a low growl a moment before Finn replied to the man's taunt. "I claim her as my bride."

"But she doesn't accept." The man laughed. The sound made Ava's skin crawl.

Finn's body tensed, his muscles going rock-hard under where she rested her hands on his biceps. "She has agreed to courtship. You have no business here."

The other elf stepped closer, ignoring the warning growls from Kellam while his gaze fixed on Ava. She started to back away but straightened her spine instead. Something told her she was safe with Finn and his guard. "My nephew has forgotten his manners. I'm Quinn, the rightful King of the Morna."

Ah, the pieces connect. Ava narrowed her gaze on Quinn and opened her mind's eye. His aura was a much darker green than Finn's, with a layer of black closest to his body. *Dark power.* The words were a whisper in her mind.

Without warning, Quinn thrust one hand toward Kellam, throwing the large bodyguard several yards into the forest. Ava gasped and flinched as Quinn gripped Finn by the neck. "I could kill you now."

No. Ava shook. Warm, electrifying energy flowed around her, fueling her fear that was now like a wildfire inside her. "Let him go."

She almost didn't recognize her own voice. The heat within her grew, and her hands began to glow.

A moment later, Quinn held up his hand and a dagger formed in it. Dread sliced through her. Before she could react, Quinn sank the blade into Finn's stomach and released him. Finn fell to the ground, coughing. Ava's heart hammered in her chest as she glanced from Finn's still form to Quinn's evil grin. "What did you do?"

She ran to Finn but didn't make it. Quinn grabbed her by the waist, tightly banded his arm around her, and held her back to his chest. His hot breath brushed against her cheek as he growled out, "Something I should have done a long time ago. Bow to your new King."

Oh, hell no. The earlier energy, or power, or whatever it was flowing around her intensified. The glowing beneath her skin turned blue, then took on an orange hue, like the color of flames. It wasn't around her, but rather inside her. Confused and desperate, she welcomed the new power and used it to try to break Quinn's hold on her. "Let. Me. Go."

As soon she grabbed his wrist and pushed at him, he cursed and let her go. She stumbled a few steps before regaining her balance and then rushed to Finn's side. Relief filled her when she saw his chest rise and fall with shallow breaths.

"Bitch!"

Quinn's snarl drew her attention up in time to see the elf storming toward them. She threw her hands up out of instinct, and an iridescent dome formed over her and Finn. *What?* Just then, Kellam barreled into Quinn. The men rolled on the ground, and then Quinn was gone, obviously teleporting away.

Ava focused on Finn. He'd lost a lot of blood. "You're not healing. Why?"

"Not enough magick. Too weak." He coughed again.

She framed his face in her hands and stared into his green eyes. Compassion mixed with a familiar sense of belonging swam in her mind and heart. Even though she didn't know Finn, she cared whether he lived or not. It was as if he died, so would she. *Odd.*

"I don't understand any of this," she whispered before leaning down to kiss him.

Warmth and magick surrounded them as their lips touched, soft at first. The energy within her lessened, and when she broke the kiss, she realized she'd transferred it to Finn somehow. His wound knitted itself closed. Within minutes, it was as if he were never hurt.

He locked gazes with her and smiled. "Thank you."

She shook her head. "I'm not sure what I did."

He took her hands and stood, bringing her with him. With a finger, he touched the shimmering dome, and it dissolved like a bubble being popped. "I'll explain inside."

Nodding, she followed him while Kellam fell in step behind them. Her body still hummed from whatever she had done. A sense of numbness settled over her. She'd reacted before she even knew what she was doing.

Once inside, Finn took her hand and led her to the parlor and closed the doors behind Kellam. "Are you all right?"

"I think so. What about you?" She pointed to his stomach where Quinn had stabbed him.

Finn offered a small smile and lifted his tunic to reveal smooth, unscarred skin. "All healed, thanks to you."

Kellam spoke from the window. "She's a Fire Elf."

Finn studied her for a long moment. "No, I think she's purely elemental. At least, that would make more sense because she is both Morna and Calim."

"I still don't want to believe it, but I can't explain what happened out there." She wrapped her arms around her waist, refusing to fall part. Not again. She'd done that once, when her parents died. And she'd vowed to be stronger.

"Come sit. Please." Finn patted the couch cushion beside him.

With a sigh, she sat. "Why didn't I have any of these powers before? And what triggered them now?"

"Simply being in this world could have triggered your magick. Like I said before, we are almost powerless in the human realm." Finn caressed her cheek.

"You burned Quinn, wounded him." Kellam glanced at her, one side of his mouth lifting in an approving smile.

Ava glanced from Kellam to Finn. "So my parents really were the elf couple that started the war."

"Yes. I know it more now than ever." Finn framed her face and pressed his lips to hers. Desire flooded her in a hot wave. But too soon, he pulled away. "And only my fated mate could share her power with me."

Her heart slammed to her feet. His fated mate? As in bride. She shook her head. "I don't think—"

He placed a finger over her lips, stopping her denial. "I will not push you. The choice is yours. But you should know that I'm willing to do anything to make you mine, including seducing you."

She was in trouble. The more time she spent with him, the harder it was getting to resist him. "Before any seducing starts. I want answers about my parents and their lives here. About you and your role as Elf King and what it would mean for me if I choose—that's a big if—to become your Queen. I want to know why your uncle wants to kill you. And now me. Can I meet the Calim?"

Finn laughed. "Slow down. You will get your answers in time. To answer your last question, we leave within the hour to meet with Willow, the Calim Queen."

Ava frowned. "I hope it's not a formal meeting." She glanced down at her tan slacks and white button-up top. Though she was dressed professionally for work, she didn't think it was proper attire to meet a Queen in.

"I will summon Fern to help you freshen up and dress." He kissed her forehead then stood. "I'll meet you in the foyer when you're ready."

Nodding, she watched Finn push a button on a small device on the table next to the sofa. Curious, she slid to the end of the couch to study the object. It appeared to be a communication device, like a call button she might find outside a building or something. *Convenient.*

She glanced back up to Finn's face, meeting his gaze. "If my father was once the Calim Prince, then who is the Queen to me?"

"She is your father's sister." He cupped her cheek. "I must go tend to something before we leave."

Offering what she hoped was a reassuring smile, she said, "Go. I'll be fine. Plus, Fern seems nice."

The green of his eyes darkened briefly before his features smoothed to express no emotion. "She is young and can be a bit...bold at times."

Ava stood and kissed his cheek. "I can handle myself and Fern. Go, take care of your business."

The corners of his lips twitched right before he dipped his head to give her a quick kiss. "I have no doubt you can."

He left the room, and Ava sighed. She'd been transported to this world for a reason. Mating the Elf King may only be a fraction of it. No, if she was whom Finn believed she was, then it was prophesied that she'd restore the magick in the kingdom. All she had to do was figure out how. Easy.

Her head began to throb. She'd been overthinking since she'd walked through that door. Yet, the sense of being overwhelmed hadn't slammed into her. Not unless burning a man counted as jumping off the ledge. She was strangely calm inside. As if a part of her *knew* she had to be there.

As for mating Finn? She didn't even want to go there. Not at the moment anyway.

The parlor doors opened, and she met the gleeful gaze of Fern. "Good afternoon, miss. Are you ready to prepare to meet the Calim Queen?"

Ava smiled and nodded. "As ready as I'll ever be." She followed the young elf through the great room to the stairs. "You know I'm going to ask you for dirty details about Finn, right?"

A giggle bubbled out of the girl. "Yes, ma'am. I have tales to share. It shall be fun to have you around."

Ditto. Ava's smile widened. She could tell that she and Fern were going to become good friends.

CHAPTER 4

Finn entered his study and headed straight to his desk. "Quinn will not let this go."

A low growl escaped Kellam as the male turned from the window. "All the more reason you shouldn't make the trip to the Calim Elves."

"It's important to Ava to know her family. And Willow is her only known relative." Even though it was the Calim who'd killed her Dark family. However, it was Willow's place to tell Ava that. "We'll take the carriage and go through the enchanted forest."

His head of security's silence told him that Kellam didn't like the plan. Well, tough shit. Finn was not going to hide. Especially from his uncle. "Have you heard from your source?"

"There is talk about a female hybrid. At first, I thought he was talking about Ava, but now I wonder if there is another." Kellam said.

Finn cut a sharp gaze to Kellam. "Another? What makes you believe that?"

"Vin says the female is evil and very powerful." Kellam sighed before continuing. "Ava may be powerful, even if she doesn't know it, but she is not evil."

Yes, Finn agreed with that. "Have you asked Willow about this female?"

Another growl rumbled from the large male. "She avoided answering by telling me to make sure you made it on time and in one piece."

If the Calim Queen wouldn't answer Kellam, then it was true. There was another half-breed among them. But why hadn't she made her presence known? And what did she want? "What do you have panned for security for the trip?"

"I'll have two guards leading the carriage and two trailing. I will ride inside with you. There is a dummy carriage leaving in about five minutes with my twin leading it." Kellam moved to the door. "I'll make sure everything is set. We should be moving soon."

Finn nodded and waved his guard off. He longed for the day when he didn't have to hide behind his guards because of the rebels. To be able to walk in the forest, free of a kill order hanging over his head.

For now, he'd bide his time. Quinn would get desperate and fuck up. When he did, Finn would be there to make sure he paid for all his sins.

Cool silk slid over Ava's skin, soothing away the heat from using magick she didn't know she possessed. After the royal blue gown had settled into place, she studied her appearance in the full-length mirror with a smile.

She looked like a renaissance princess with a modern twist. The high waist accented her breasts perfectly, she noted with a half-smile. She lifted her arms to see the full effect of the bell sleeves. *Nice.*

Fern came into view from behind her in the mirror. "If I am an elf, why don't I have the pointed ears?"

With a gleam in her eyes, Fern brushed Ava's hair back, revealing her left ear. When the female touched the top, a ripple formed around Ava and made her shiver. Blinking once, she stared at her reflection in awe as Fern explained. "Your parents must have placed a glamour spell on you."

No shit. Ava didn't only have pointed ears, but her skin also shimmered with a mixture of light and dark. "Why would they not tell me?"

Fern fell quiet and walked away from the mirror. Ava turned and watched her tidy up the room. "Fern. Answer the question."

"I'm not sure. Finn should be the one to tell you."

Ava closed her eyes and took slow breaths before responding. "Finn says my life is in danger now that I'm here."

Fern nodded. "The rebels want you dead. They vowed when the seer predicted your arrival to kill you. Rumor says they are plotting to claim the thrones of both the Light and Dark kingdoms."

Quinn's face flashed in Ava's mind. It was clear the male didn't like the fact that Finn was King. "Is Quinn a rebel?"

"Yes, ma'am. He's the leader." The words were spoken low, like she didn't want to talk about it. When Fern glanced back at her, she smiled wide. "Now that your glamour is gone, you are ready to meet your aunt."

"My aunt? Oh, yes. The Calim Queen."

Fern nodded. "She is beautiful and nice. You will love her."

Ava had a family. Well, at least an aunt. "What do you know about my mom's family?"

Again Fern turned away from her, like she had with the last question she didn't want to answer. Ava decided to let it go and save the questions for Finn. "Never mind. You're uncomfortable."

"No. That's not it. I never knew your mom, but my mom did. She worked here in the palace." Fern gathered up Ava's clothes and headed to the door. "After your parents left and war broke out, your mother's family were captured and killed."

Ava's heart sank and broke all over again. The loss of both of her parents rose up, bringing the pain front and center. Tears stung her eyes. "Thank you for being honest with me."

"I'm sorry." Fern lingered at the door as if unsure what to do.

"Don't be." Ava wiped her eyes and took a deep breath, then released it in a rush. "We should get going. I'm sure Finn is waiting."

And Ava wanted to meet Willow.

With a nod, Fern led her down to the foyer where Finn waited patiently. He wore a black, high-low jacket over a tan tunic. When he faced her completely, she sucked in a breath at how handsome he was with his hair hanging loose around his shoulders. Then he smiled, and Ava swore her knees would give out.

"You are beautiful," he said and offered his hand to her.

She placed her hand in his. "I'm not sure about the ears and the shimmer."

When he gave a gentle tug of her hand, she stumbled into him. "It will take some time to get used to, I suppose. Just promise me you'll let me know when you are unhappy."

"You don't have to worry about that. I'm good at expressing my unhappiness." She laughed, and suddenly, her nerves sent a zap of worry through her. She was the love child of the couple who'd started a war. Finn's warning of being in danger finally sank in. The rebels wanted her dead. Who knew how many others resented her parents.

Finn smoothed her brow with his fingers. "You have nothing to fear. After I announce the wedding, it will be against the law to harm you, punishable by death."

Dread and shock stilled her heart for a brief moment. "Wait. I didn't agree to marry you."

A crooked smile formed on his sensual mouth, and a spark of knowing twinkled in his emerald gaze. "Oh, but you will."

Will I? "You are so sure of yourself."

"Yes. I always get what I want."

She had no doubt of that. Every minute she spent with him, she found it harder and harder to remember why she had to return home. And really, what was holding her to one place or another? However, if it meant learning more about her parents and the life they'd hidden from her, she was intrigued enough to stick around. Plus, Finn sparked a desire she'd never felt toward anyone before. "We'll see," she teased.

A bright flash rippled across the irises of his green eyes as a grin played on his face. "Challenge accepted." He offered his elbow to her. "We shouldn't keep Willow waiting."

Looping her arm with his, she sighed. "I'm ready."

He led her out the door to the horse-drawn carriage waiting for them in the circular gravel driveway. Her heart thumped in her head as she allowed Finn to help her into the carriage. Wanting to focus on one thing at a time, she said, "I guess there are no cars here."

"Cars?"

His drawn brows and curious glance at her told her the answer was no. "I didn't think so. Cars are motorized vehicles that run on gas and oil."

He smiled. "Yes, I've heard of them. We don't need such things here. We are creatures of nature, after all."

Now that she thought about it, she did feel more clear-headed and at ease. No noise, no pollution. Just her and the natural setting of the forest. It was enchanting in more ways than she'd dreamed. "Would it be possible for a tour of your kingdom?"

His hands fisted in his lap. After a few moments, he uncurled his hands and covered one of hers. "I would love to show you my kingdom, but—"

She placed a finger over his lips, halting him in mid-sentence. "I didn't mean right now. I can wait until the threat on my life is over."

"You are staying?"

A laugh escaped her. "Not so fast. I'm not sure I belong here, but I will help you in any way I can. Plus, my parents are from here, apparently, and I want to know everything about their life here."

"Fair enough." He linked their fingers and added, "Would you join me for a late-night stroll after we return?"

Giddiness rose within her. "I'd love that."

She glanced out the small window with a smile. Peace had settled over her as if she had finally found where she belonged. As far as marrying the Morna King? Well, he would have to do some serious wooing.

The carriage rolled to a stop in front of a beautiful, white and gold mansion. Rose vines with multi-colored blooms crawled up the sides. A large staircase spilled from the center of the front of the house, meeting the gravel of the driveway. "It's beautiful."

"It's okay."

Ava glanced at him and noted the semi-smile on his lips. "It's beyond beautiful to me. In fact, this whole place is."

He leaned over so his lips brushed against her ear and whispered, "I'll have you begging to stay before the week is up."

Heat pooled in her abdomen. She sucked in her bottom lip before saying, "You really are sure of yourself."

The green in his eyes darkened and he leaned into her. Their gazes locked, intensifying the wildfire inside her. Then she lowered her eyes to his lips. What she wouldn't do for a proper kiss in that moment.

Just then, a hint of awareness brushed against her subconscious, and Finn broke the eye contact to glare out the window. "Your aunt grows impatient."

Ava glanced behind her. At the top of the large staircase, stood a woman she'd know anywhere, yet had never met. With long, blonde hair the color of spun gold, the Calim Queen was beautiful. The lavender gown she wore fell to the ground and pooled into a train, spreading out behind her. She also looked too much like Ava's father to be anyone but his sister.

Tears filled Ava's eyes, and instantly she opened the carriage and ran up the stairs. When she reached the top, she threw her arms around Willow. Footsteps closed in from all directions, but Ava didn't care. Suddenly, they stopped, making Ava glance up. Willow had her hand up as if to call off the guards, but she didn't need to. They stared at Ava in awe.

"What's going on?"

Willow framed her face and smiled. "I didn't tell them you were coming. I wanted it to be a surprise." The Queen turned to the guard closest to her. "We'll take our tea in the gardens, privately."

The large elfin male nodded then rattled off orders to the others. After they'd disappeared, Willow looped an arm with Ava's and greeted Finn and Kellam. "Does he have to hover?"

Finn glanced at Kellam, who then let out a growl before returning to the carriage. Turning his attention back to Willow, Finn bowed and held out his hand. "Hovering is his specialty."

Willow laughed. "Thank you for bringing her to me."

Finn flicked a glance to Ava. "There is much we need to discuss."

"Yes. Come." Willow descended the stairs, still holding on to Ava's arm. "We won't be disturbed. Plus, the gardens are enchanted to keep unwanted guests out."

Ava glanced at Finn, worried that Willow had gotten uninvited guests like they had earlier. Finn kept his features emotionless. She'd have to ask him how he did that.

When they approached the gardens, all her worries seemed to mute to a low hum in the back of her mind. The fragrance of gardenias and lilies filled the air. The sense of calm circled around her. Yet, Ava couldn't stop her fidgeting as she sat between Willow and Finn at a white circular table in a small courtyard. Questions whirled in her mind. So much had been opened up to her in the short time she'd been in their world, and she didn't know where to start.

Finally, Willow spoke as if knowing what she needed. "I see both of your parents in you."

"Tell me about them?"

Willow smiled. "They were so in love. From the moment they met. Jandar planned their escape before asking your mother."

"How did they meet?" Ava relaxed a little and sat back in her seat.

"I'm not sure of the details. Jan said he met her in the neutral area between the kingdoms. Faylan was hunting, unaware she was being watched. At least, that was Jandar's tale." Willow's smile faded. "His eyes lit up at the mention of her. I was the only one he could tell. We were twins, after all."

Sadness washed over Ava and mixed with her own grief, that of losing the only two people she'd ever cared about. "Why was it forbidden for a Morna and Calim to fall in love?"

"My father was a harsh ruler and believed the two kingdoms should never have any kind of relations. Growing up, Jan and I were taught to accept it as the law. When we got older, we realized it as our father's own prejudice against our Dark cousins." Willow let out a sigh before sipping her tea. "When Jandar left our realm with Faylan, Father was beyond furious and blamed the Morna for turning his only son against his kingdom."

Ava's heart broke for Willow and everyone in Edra. "Then war broke out."

Willow nodded. "And both sides hoarded power to use on the other. After years of battles, the magick faded. Then, my father helped Quinn create a plague." She paused briefly. "I'd had enough of the war and the sickness spreading over the land. I drove a sword through my father's heart and claimed his throne."

With a gasp, Ava reached out to her aunt. "Oh, I'm so sorry."

Willow took her hand and held it. She opened her mouth, then moved her gaze to Finn, narrowing her eyes at him. Ava wondered what the Calim Queen saw or sensed. Returning her gaze back to Ava, Willow frowned. "You've begun the bonding."

The bonding? "What?" Confusion stirred up her fear of the unknown.

Finn spoke in a flat tone. "Your grandmother was a seer. Willow has the gift."

That still didn't answer Ava's question. Before she could ask again, Willow said, "When you saved Finn's life, you started the bonding. It's the first step to mating or getting married."

Ava tugged her hand away from her aunt and sat back in her chair again. Uncertainty swirled inside her gut. "What does that mean?"

Finn dropped his shoulders and faced her, his face full of compassion and worry. "Nothing is set until we go through with the ceremony and complete the ritual. I would never force it on you."

"Yet, you didn't tell me it had started. That I started it?"

She stood, and Finn followed. "I said you being able to heal me meant we were true mates. Nothing has started. Unless you want it to."

Ava glared at him. "So it's my fault?"

Willow cleared her throat as if to remind them she was still there. "It is no one's fault but the Fates. However, there are bigger issues we must discuss." When Ava sat back down, Willow continued. "Ava will be a target for the rebels. Your uncle won't stop until he has your throne."

Finn let out a growl-like sound from his throat. "Quinn will be disappointed. He will not win."

Willow picked up her teacup and tilted it toward Ava. "Not with her by your side. However, he has found Sana—the other hybrid female—and plans to mate with her."

Confused, Ava glanced from Willow to Finn. The two of them clearly knew what was going on, but neither was offering any explanations. "Who is Sana, and why do we care if she mates Quinn?"

After a long silence that threatened Ava's sanity, Willow spoke. "Sana is your half-sister. She was born days before your parents escaped to the human world."

"Half-sister? Then she is not from my father? I can't believe my mother was unfaithful." The sadness in Willow's blue gaze soured Ava's stomach. "What happened?"

"I don't know all the details. I didn't know Sana existed until a few weeks ago. My gift of Sight only shows me the future, not the past." The Queen paused as if the mention of Sana upset her more than she wanted to show. "She is like you; half Calim and half Morna. Rumors drifted on the wind that your mother had been raped by my father's guards. A punishment for ruining the Calim Prince."

Tears welled up in Willow's eyes, breaking Ava's heart. Taking a breath and wanting to change the subject, she searched her mind for a question not involving her parents. She'd find out more about her mother later. Someone in the Morna kingdom would know her mother. Or she could hunt down Sana for a little Q&A. "How am I supposed to *set things right*?"

A smile lit up Willow's face. "You will come forward to all the people, win their trust and love, and then restore the Light and Dark magicks of the land. In turn, you will unite both kingdoms."

That didn't answer her question. "How am I to restore the magick?"

"Only you will know when the time is right. I will say it comes from your heart, and it is something you must learn on your own." Willow stood and scanned the area. "You must stay for dinner."

Ava and Finn nodded at the same time. Something told Ava that it was going to be a long and painful journey. The question of the decade was, would she survive it?

CHAPTER 5

Ava stepped out onto the green lawn that seemed to stretch out for acres behind Finn's large estate. They'd returned an hour ago from the Calim kingdom. Ava had told Finn she was tired, but when she got to her room, she couldn't rest. Too much going through her mind.

Her main concern was how she had not thought about home or anyone there. Was she being too insensitive about Jeff's death and Alice? Of course, the widow had stolen from her.

"A pebble for your thoughts."

Finn's rich, slightly accented voice smoothed over her from behind. It was so hard to deny him, or stay away from him. "I'm a little restless, and thought some night air would help."

He came to stand next to her then linked their hands together. "You are troubled."

"Before I found the skeleton key and entered this world, I found out that my business partner was killed. I was sadder for his wife than myself. Does it make me a horrible person that I don't mourn his death?" Once the words had left her mouth, she realized that she hadn't grieved for her parents either. Well not for a long period of time. Sure, she was sad—she'd even cried—when they died, but she didn't mourn for them like other people did. Like *humans* did.

"We don't see death as an end. It is the beginning of their next journey. So no, you are not a horrible being." Finn faced her and placed her hand over his heart. "I miss my parents every day, but I know I will meet them again. If not in the afterlife, then in the next one."

That is how she felt, but didn't know how to explain it. "I guess I kind of knew something was going to happen. I mean, Jeff had been acting strangely for a few weeks before his death. I guess it was why I'd started to pull away from the business, like I was looking for something else."

Finn began to walk, tugging her along with him. "I'm not surprised you have strong intuition. You could have gotten it from your grandmother on your father's side."

Ava nodded. Now that she knew that her father's mother was a seer, a lot of things made sense to her. "Why was the Calim King unforgiving? I mean, he was a Calim Elf."

"The differences between the Calim and the Morna are not good versus bad. It's in our magick. The Calim get their powers from the sun and all things ruled by it. My people and I are ruled by the magick of the moon, the darkness." Finn glanced at her briefly. She swore she saw a flash of concern in his eyes. It was his next words that confirmed what she saw. "You are both. Therefore, you get your powers from both the sun and the moon."

"Making me more powerful than any elf alive." Suddenly, she wasn't sure she wanted to be there anymore. "No wonder your uncle wants me dead."

"Sana is also a hybrid. And she's had her whole life to hone her powers." Finn spoke low, and his tone had a hint of a tremble to it.

"Who says I haven't? I mean, I may have lived in the human realm, but I can't believe my parents would leave me defenseless. Even though they lied to me about who I am."

With a gentle tug, Finn pulled her into his warm arms and stopped walking. "They wouldn't. They would make sure you had what you needed. My guess is they might have prepared you all along, waiting for the day they would reveal everything."

Ava let out a sigh. He was right, but she was too tired to think anymore about it. "Tell me about your childhood."

"I was born months before the war broke out. Most of my life was spent in a safe shelter in the Wastelands, where I trained until I was old enough to fight in the war." He smiled at her, apparently sensing her horror at his upbringing. "We were at war. Besides, all our children are trained at a young age to fight, hunt, and survive."

She wasn't sure she liked the idea but let it go for now. "So I guess you didn't have time for fun."

"I did. It wasn't always work. But life in the Wastelands is very different."

"Are they as dark and dead as they sound?"

Finn chuckled. "Yes. The Calim are powerless there, for there is no sun and very little light."

Ava frowned. "The perfect place to hide your children and females during a war."

"I regret nothing about my childhood. Besides, the training aided me while claiming the throne. I defeated my uncle then, and will again." A flash of inner light, or was it more of a glow, lit up his emerald eyes. He turned away from her too fast for her to study his reaction. "Quinn warned me when I banned him from my kingdom that he would return and challenge me."

Ava huffed out a low growl. "That man...er elf...will not rule. He's evil."

Finn faced her again, a seductive smile curving his lips. "Rule with me. Say yes and be my Queen." He snaked an arm around her and tugged her close so their bodies meshed together. "The human world isn't your home. Edra is."

She studied him for several long moments. There was nothing waiting for her return. Her career was ruined, and she'd have to start over anyway. However, there was something in his tone that told her he wasn't sharing everything. "What are you not saying?"

He closed his eyes briefly and inhaled slowly, releasing the breath just as slow. "I must take a bride to keep the throne. They were Quinn's last words when he left."

"Like a curse?"

He nodded. "A challenge, threat, whatever you want to call it."

Crossing her arms, she scanned his features. "With me here, you fear he'll make good on his word to claim the throne?"

"Especially if he indeed marries Sana. He'll be too powerful to defeat."

The power the two elves would form after the union would be too great for Finn to fight alone. He needed Ava to protect his throne and people. Willow did say that Ava had already started the bonding. And the more she got to know Finn, the more she wanted to be a part of his world and life. Plus, Edra was her parents' home. "What would being your Queen mean for me?"

"You would rule by my side, be loved by our people, and become the most powerful elf in Edra."

She smiled, hearing the teasing tone of his voice as he said the last part of that statement. "I don't want power."

He closed the gap between them and heat rose within her. "That's what makes you the perfect Queen." He dipped his head and pressed his lips to hers. An inferno raged to life in her core, then spread throughout her body.

Pleasure consumed her, making it hard to think straight. In that moment, she wanted him like she'd wanted no other. It was crazy. She didn't believe in instalove, but there was no denying the feeling that she belonged to him, in this place.

She let out a soft groan as he broke the kiss. A dark presence touched her awareness. Even the hair on her body stood on end. Whirling around, she came face-to-face with Quinn and a female. The female looked a little like Ava's mom, telling her that this was her sister. However, it was obvious it wasn't going to be a happy family reunion. Sana was so full of hate, anger, and regret that she'd allowed it to darken her heart. Her aura said it all.

"We finally meet, sister." Sana's cool taunt was spoken on a chuckle.

Ava narrowed her eyes, which she never took off Sana, because deep down, Ava knew her sister was the real threat. "He's just using you."

It was a weak attempt to fire back at her, but it was the first thing that popped into Ava's mind. Suddenly, she heard Sana speak, but the female's mouth never moved. The words were sent telepathically, for Ava's ears only. "You are wrong. It is I who am using him."

Visions and images of the Calim palace consumed by flames flashed in Ava's mind. An army of Morna storming the kingdom, killing everyone in their path. Bodies of the Calim littering the forest floor and village streets... The images flashed faster and faster through the horrid event. A future event where Sana controlled an army to wipe out the Calim.

The images cut off abruptly, leaving Ava to stumble a step backwards. Finn touched her lower back with his hand, but it did nothing to soothe the rage building inside her. Cutting her evil sister a glare, Ava snarled, "You will not get away with it."

If the bitch could get inside my head, then I can get in hers. Ava focused and sent her a message, checking to see if she could telepathically communicate with Sana. "*I will not allow you to hurt anyone.*"

A raise of a brow told Ava she was heard. Good. "*You are weak, little sister. I've had my whole life to strengthen my powers, while you were hidden in the human realm.*"

Sana didn't hide her jealousy very well. Ava smirked. Gotcha. "*I'm sure you had a good upbringing. What made your heart so dark?*"

Rage swirled around Sana a moment before she charged at Ava, much too fast for her to track. Sana tackled her to the ground before a shimmering bubble formed around them, leaving out the men. Ava glanced to Finn and spotted fear in his green depths. Flicking her attention back to Sana, who had her pinned to the ground, Ava grabbed her sister's face and cupped her head while staring into her eyes. Flashes of Sana's childhood ran through Ava's mind.

"You were loved."

Sana snarled and gripped Ava's throat. "I was thrown away like trash. My own mother ordered me to be killed."

Ava didn't react to Sana's outburst. Instead, she continued to sift through Sana's memories. As soon as she touched on a name, like a whisper in her sister's mind, Sana released her and jerked away from Ava. She then stormed toward Quinn, breaking the circle Ava had created around them.

A moment later, the two dematerialized.

Finn was at her side in an instant, helping her up. "Are you okay?"

Ava nodded. "I'm telepathic."

"Only with family. It's common among close families to develop the power." Finn ran his hands up her arms, then around her back as if searching for injuries. "Did she hurt you?"

"Only my heart." Ava hugged him close. "While Quinn wants your throne, Sana wants all the Calim dead. Let's go find Kellam and then I'll explain."

They had to find a way to stop Sana before she made good on her threat. Because Ava couldn't allow the future Sana had showed her to come true. Sana and Quinn had to be stopped. And Ava was going to make it happen.

CHAPTER 6

Finn led Ava and Kellam into the study as fury mixed with confusion filled his head. His uncle had gone too far by bringing Sana to the palace. He turned to Ava at the soft click of the door. Before he could speak, she held up a hand. "They have to be stopped. Sana shared her vision of the future. She plans to kill Willow and destroy the Calim kingdom. The bitch is crazy."

Ava started pacing, anxiety rolling off her in waves. Finn reined in his own fears and anger. "What else did she say to you? Show to you?"

Ava shook her head. "Nothing. But I did get the name of someone. A woman. Kenia."

"Don't know the name." Finn met Kellam's stare. The male shook his head.

"I need to find someone who knows about Sana's birth. Like where she was taken. Who raised her? Something tells me it's this Kenia woman." Ava paced as her words faded to a mumble as if she were trying to figure it out on her own. Then she stopped and faced Finn. "Fern said her mother worked with my mother in the palace."

That was news to him since he'd been a baby when the war broke out. He moved to his desk and pressed the call button that would send his message to all the staff's earpieces. "Fern, I request your presence in my study."

Ava hugged her waist, but Finn sensed the electrifying power around her, angry and waiting to be unleashed. Her hands fisted as she spoke. "She has to be stopped. I keep seeing the Calim kingdom destroyed. Buildings burned to the ground, the elves...all dead." A sob escaped her, breaking Finn's heart.

He went to her and drew her into his arms. "Shh, that will not happen. We will stop her." He met Kellam's pissed-off gaze. "Contact Willow and let her know she is also a target."

Kellam gave a short nod and left the room.

A moment later, Fern entered. Finn offered her a gentle smile. "Can you call your mom on video conference? We have some questions to ask about Ava's mother."

With a quick glance to Ava, Fern nodded. "Yes, my lord." Then she moved to the monitor on the wall between the bookshelves and touched the screen. It fired to life, revealing the keypad to dial out. After she'd typed in her mother's number, Fern stepped aside.

Crystal answered on the first ring, her face lit up with a bright grin until she noted Finn. She forced a smile, but worry still creased her forehead. "My lord." Then she saw Ava and gasped. "Ava."

It was a whisper, but he heard it and knew that Crystal indeed knew Faylan well enough to know her secrets. At least, he hoped Crystal did. "Cry, I hope you are well. We are sorry to bother you, but hoped you could give us information about Faylan and the child she ordered to be killed."

A frown wiped away Crystal's happy greeting. She glanced away from the screen as if wishing she had never answered the call. After another moment, Ava said, "Anything you can tell me about my mother will be greatly appreciated."

"The child from her rape is alive and has targeted the Calim Queen for assassination," Finn offered in hopes of swaying Crystal to volunteer what she knew.

With a heavy sigh, Crystal dropped her shoulders and lifted her gaze back to Finn. Sadness moved into her grey gaze like storm clouds. "Faylan was so in love with Jandar, and he with her. The day before her rape, she'd told me Jandar had proposed marriage. She said he would do anything to be with her, even denounce the throne."

Crystal's gaze fell slightly and a single tear rolled down her cheek. Ava moved closer to Finn, and he linked their fingers together. "Cry, please continue."

"After the rape, Faylan retreated to her quarters and wouldn't talk to anyone, not even me at first. When she found out she was pregnant, she left the palace and went to stay with her aunt in the Wastelands." A sob escaped her. "It doesn't surprise me that she'd order the child be put to death. Anyway, it'd been a year since I'd seen her when she snuck into the palace to say her goodbyes. She said she and Jandar were leaving Edra."

Ava tensed slight and asked, "What was her aunt's name?"

Yes, Finn wondered about that, too.

"Kenia."

Ava faced him, hope lighting up her face. "We have to go to the Wastelands."

His first instinct was to say no, that he wasn't going to risk her life by taking her to the darkest and most dangerous place in Edra. However, he couldn't deny her her family, and they did need to find out more about Sana. He nodded to Crystal. "Thank you. You need to visit the palace more often."

Crystal smiled. "I will." The smile faded. "My lord, should I be concerned?"

"Not yet. Fern can keep you updated."

"Thank you." Crystal ended the call.

Finn tugged Ava to the sofa and sat down. "The Wastelands isn't what it used to be. Many of the rebels live there, and they will capture and kill anyone loyal to Willow and me. We will need to travel with a guard or two and in disguise."

"When do we leave?"

Squeezing her hands gently, he shook his head. Ava should be protected, not heading off into danger. He let out a soft chuckle. He sounded like Kellam trying to talk him out of a mission. And Finn wouldn't listen to his guard any more than Ava would him. "Right after I brief you on the Wastelands. You must do as I say."

"The two of you will listen to me." Kellam marched into the room, a snarl in his voice and his glare pinned on Finn. "The Wastelands are filled with creatures that feed on others' misery and pain. It's like what the humans call hell, the Underworld, the demon realm."

Finn shrugged. "It's dark and cold." He took Ava's hands in his, drawing her attention to him. She needed to understand that she could come out of there a changed female. "You will need to tap into your Dark power more because your Light half will not be able to aid you."

"Because there is no sun. I got it." Ava inhaled, then released it slowly. "I need to talk with Kenia and find out everything I can about Sana. I will not allow her to destroy the Calim kingdom."

Finn stood and nodded to Fern, who stood silently by the door, waiting for instructions. "Please assist Ava with finding a proper outfit for our journey. And don't mention to anyone where we have gone."

Fern bowed and motioned to Ava. "Miss."

After a few moments, Ava left with Fern. Finn faced Kellam. "I will borrow clothes from one of the staff. I only want you and one other guard with us."

"The less, the better." Kellam stalked to the door, then glanced at Finn from over his shoulder. "Willow fears we don't have too much time."

Finn nodded. Sana's energy was full of anger and darkness, with a little desperation in her scent. She would make a mistake, but not before destroying as many lives as she could. He hoped they could stop her before losing everything he'd fought so hard for.

The Wastelands were everything that Ava imagined. There was no green grass or leaves on any of the trees. Even though there was no sun, it wasn't truly dark. It was like being in a place stuck in twilight.

"How do we find her?" Ava was so fixated on stopping Sana from her evil plot, she hadn't thought things through fully. However, Finn seemed confident. Did he know how to find Kenia?

He brought his horse to a stop next to hers. "She is your great-aunt. You can sense her. Just focus on her name and your mother's face, then ask the elements around you to guide you."

Ah, she knew how to do that. Her mother had taught her to listen to the wind for its secrets. A smile spread her lips. *Thanks, Mom.*

Closing her eyes, she stretched out her senses, searching her surroundings. Nothing came to her. No whispers, no magick. "The air feels neutral. It's almost like we are stuck in between Light and Dark."

"It is possible. Many things have changed over the years." Finn's tone was matter-of-fact. "If that is true, you should be able to use either side of your power or a combination of the two."

Kellam let out a breathy growl. "Come, I know someone who owes me a favor. We can see if she can tell us anything about Kenia."

The guard steered his horse to the east. Finn and Ava followed, and the other guard—Ava couldn't remember his name—trailed behind them. All the while, Ava kept trying to connect to her great-aunt. Nothing she did seemed to work. It was as if her newfound powers didn't work in the Wastelands.

"I don't think my magick works here," she whispered to Finn.

"Hmm. Something is not right." His tone was low, and the moment the words left his lips, she picked up on a heavy energy.

"What is that?" Fear burned her gut and made her heart rate increase.

Before Finn had a chance to answer her, a large, hairy beast with bat-like wings dropped out of the sky onto the path in front of them. Once the thing lowered its wings, she noted the Dark Elf on its back. His skin shimmered with red and gold, beautiful, yet deadly.

"Well, what do we have here? King Finn. I think you took a wrong turn." The male snarled at Finn, then glanced to Ava. His eyes rounded in surprise. "Looks like Quinn has been withholding information. The hybrid child has returned."

Kellam and the other guard moved in front of Finn and Ava protectively. Kellam said, "I'd advise you to move on your way and forget about seeing us here. This is not rebel land, you have no business here."

"You are wrong, demon, it is you who don't belong."

The guard beside Kellam growled and threw a fireball at the elf, but it missed him. In turn, the evil male withdrew a bow and arrow from his back and fired much too fast for Ava to track with her eyes. The arrow hit the guard in the chest, killing him instantly.

Before she knew it, Kellam swung around and slapped her horse on the rump, sending the creature speeding off into the dark forest around them. Oh, no. They would not send her off while they got themselves killed.

Come on magick, don't fail me now. Remembering what Finn had said at the palace about using her Dark side more, Ava called to the darkness, willing the magick of night and the moon to give her strength. Power started to build in her veins like warm water, heating as the energy grew stronger.

Thank you, moon mother. She turned her horse around and charged back toward the path. The males were off their horses. Finn fought the evil elf while Kellam battled the large, winged beast. Neither one were equally matched to the other. Dread almost made her lose the hold on the power she'd built. Almost.

Calling to the elements of air and fire, she created a small cyclone of flames and wind, then sent it swirling between them, not really trying to hit either group of fighters. It caught the attention of the rebel elf, which was what she had hoped for.

He smirked and stalked toward her after hitting Finn with some kind of energy ball. Ava's heart dropped to her feet, and she screamed out, "No." When Finn's chest rose and fell in labored breaths, Ava focused on the rebel. The bastard was going to pay.

"I see you've found your backbone."

His taunt did nothing but fuel her fury. She willed a bow and arrow to her hands. A smile lifted her lips as she set up for her shot. Right before she released the arrow, the rebel rushed her, knocking them both to the ground. He straddled her with his hand around her throat. Her breathing came in gasps.

"Still too slow. Like a human."

She tried to throw him off, but he was too heavy. From the corner of her eye, she spotted Finn still lying on the ground, barely moving. And she didn't know where Kellam was. He and the beast had taken their battle into the forest.

A moment later, the elf gasped, his back arching before his grip loosened around her neck and he fell to the ground next to her. A female stood at Ava's feet with a sword in her hand. She nodded to Ava. "You've been looking for me?"

Kenia.

Ava rolled to her side then stood. "I'm Ava Green—"

"I know who you are." Kenia's voice softened, and she glanced to Finn and frowned. "Fucking rebels. They've been told to stay away from this part of the Wastelands."

Kellam emerged from the forest, his clothes blood-soaked, and a gash over his right eye. "Why are they here?"

Kenia glared at him then looked at Ava when she answered. "They are trying to build armies, take over areas they don't own and force the weak to fight for their cause." She pointed to Finn and added, "Bring him to my place. Others will be here any moment."

Kellam went to Finn and picked him up, then motioned Ava to follow Kenia. She did as directed. Her great-aunt didn't seem pleased to see them. Well, that was too bad. Ava came for information, and that was what she was going to get.

One way or another.

CHAPTER 7

Ava watched Kenia as she poured herbal tea into cups, and then carried one to her. Accepting the tea, Ava said, "Thank you."

"Your mother and I were close. Like sisters. So it was natural for her to come to me after the attack." Kenia sat down on the love seat next to Ava.

With a quick glance to Finn stretched out on the couch across from them, Ava nodded. "You know why I'm here." It wasn't a question, and she was glad she didn't have to explain anything or ask questions to confirm what Willow had said about the rape.

"I use the water and fire elements to see into the future and past. It's not as efficient as being a seer like your grandmother, but I get by. Know when the bastard rebels are headed my way." Kenia lifted her gaze to Finn as she continued. "I'm one of the few in the Wastelands who is still loyal to the Morna King."

"Sana needs to be stopped," Kellam said from the bay window behind them.

Kenia closed her eyes and sat back. "There are many nights, especially recently, that I question my own judgment. Mainly why I didn't kill the child as Faylan wanted."

"I couldn't have killed a baby either." Ava's heart hurt to think about it. Although she understood that keeping Sana would have been a reminder of what the Calim had done to her mother.

"When I decided to raise Sana myself, I never dreamed she would allow hate into her heart as she did. It has consumed her." Kenia stood and moved to a small desk next to the fireplace. "Sana became too unpredictable and too powerful. Nothing I did or said would change her mind about seeking her revenge. She left several months ago, and I haven't heard from her since."

Kenia pulled something out of a hidden compartment in the desk and brought it to Ava. She placed an onyx about the size of a quarter in Ava's palm. "This will aid you when you need it most. Sana wants nothing more than to destroy everything your parents love, including you and your mate."

Fury boiled in Ava's soul. No one would touch Finn, or anyone else for that matter. The stone in her hand began to warm. "She won't get away with any of it. I'll stop her in any way I must."

Kenia nodded, sadness rolling off her. "You may depend on the sun and moon for your magick, but your power also comes from your heart, your emotions. Your passion. You can do anything you desire."

Finn let out a groan and slowly sat up. Without a second thought, Ava rushed to his side. "How do you feel?"

"Never better." He gave her a weak smile.

"Liar," she said playfully, but Ava sensed his fatigue and eagerness to go home. Plus, the dark, inky air of the Wastelands was starting to weigh on her. After meeting Kellam's gaze, she turned to Kenia. "Thank you for your help."

Kenia held out her hands, and Ava took them. "Your mom would be proud of how strong you've grown. Just remember that together you two are much stronger."

Ava followed her aunt's gaze to Finn. Her intuition said Kenia was talking about the bond. Facing her great-aunt again, Ava pulled her into a tight hug. "When this is over, we must catch up. There is so much I want to know."

"Sure, baby. Just call on me anytime." Kenia kissed her on the cheek.

"Ava." Kellam's soft tone pulled her back to the issue at hand.

She followed Kellam to the door then stopped when Kenia spoke. "I have a teleporter in my store room. You could use that to get the King back home safely. I'll make sure your horses are returned within a few days."

Kellam gave a short nod and turned to follow Kenia to the back of the house. Ava hugged her one last time before entering the door that Kenia called a teleporter. It actually looked similar to the door that Ava had used to enter this world. Yet the energy was different, darker.

Once back at the palace, Finn appeared to feel better. His color was back to normal. Well, normal for him.

Ava, on the other hand, had a lot going through her mind. Her great-aunt's words were in the forefront of her mind.

"What is it?" Finn asked and caressed her cheek.

She shrugged. "Kenia said that we'd be stronger together."

He dropped his hand to grip hers. "Yes, a marriage bond would enable each of us to use the other's power. We could also combine our magicks."

Making them the most powerful couple in Edra. Just as long as Quinn and Sana didn't bond, which would be just what they would do to destroy the kingdoms.

Making eye contact with Finn, she announced, "I will marry you and bind my life to yours."

His lips lifted in a smile while his brows dipped in a frown. "You don't have to do it. I mean, I want you to say yes because I know you are mine. The one I've waited for to rule by my side. But I don't want you to do anything you are not ready for."

"I have nothing in the human realm. Without my parents, I've just been existing. Here, with you, I feel alive. I have a purpose." She kissed him.

He released a low groan and wrapped his arms around her, drawing her closer to him. He licked the seam of her lips, and she opened for him. Her body ached for his touch, to feel his skin against hers.

Breaking the kiss, Finn framed her face in his hands, his green eyes lit up with passion. "Are you sure? You're not doing it to stop my uncle and your sister?"

"Yes, I'm sure. Stopping them once and for all is just a bonus." She hugged him close. "I can't explain it. I've never felt like this with anyone. It's like I know I belong here. Everything in my life is making sense, and I'm finally home."

"Once we bond, there is no undoing it as long as both of us are still alive."

"Then I'll have to kill you when I'm done with you," she teased.

He chuckled as he scooped her up in his arms and moved to the stairs. "The bond has already begun from when you shared your magick with me to save my life. All we have to do is open our hearts and minds to one another while making love. The magick will take care of the rest."

"Ah, so this whole thing is just to get me in the sack?"

"Of course."

She laughed and relished the thought of pretending for one night that she wasn't being chased by people who wanted her dead. *No, tonight I'm all Finn's. We'll deal with reality in the morning.*

He kicked the door to his room open and carried her to his bed. Her stomach felt like a hundred hummingbirds were fluttering inside. She wasn't a virgin, but she'd never felt this turned on or nervous in her life.

Laying her down on the cool sheet, he kissed her lips and moved to trail kisses across her jawline to her neck. Tingles of desire raced over her skin and burned in her core. When he lifted his head, his eyes seemed to glow.

After urging her to sit up, he gripped the hem of her tunic and lifted it over her head. Then, with slow, teasing motions he pulled her leggings and panties off. Being bare to him amped up her arousal. Her sex pulsed with need, and she had to fight to keep from touching herself. No, she wanted him to touch her, pleasure her.

As if knowing what she craved, he crawled back on the bed and placed his hands on her thighs, gently urging her to spread her legs. She complied, opening up for him. When his lips touched her core, she sucked in a breath and closed her eyes briefly, rocking her hips in time with his very talented tongue.

He lifted his head and held her gaze as he slid one hand up her thigh to finger the little bundle of nerves. Spreading her lips, his teased her with his tongue before he slid two fingers inside her. A moan escaped. Never in her life had she ever felt so much pleasure.

He covered her fully with his mouth as he pumped his fingers in and out of her pussy. Their energies mingled, and his power wrapped around her. Just when she thought she would burst from the mounting passion, he lifted his head and moved up her body with his fingers still inside her, his thumb replacing his tongue. "I want to hold you when you come," he whispered in her ear, and then kissed her neck.

Ava wrapped her arms around his neck and buried her hands in his hair, bringing his mouth to hers. The pleasure built as he moved his fingers in and out of her while his thumb rubbed her clit until the convulsing wave of an orgasm overtook her.

After the last shudder had left her body, Finn pulled away from her, slid backwards off the bed, and smiled at her groans of protest. Their eyes locked and stayed fixed on each other as he removed his pants. Gods he was beautiful. And rock-hard, she noted as he removed his clothes.

His lips lifted as he settled between her legs, positioning his cock at her entrance. Before giving her what she wanted, he reclaimed her mouth. He pushed his tongue between her lips so it could dance with hers. Heat spread through her, and she was growing impatient to have him inside her.

She raised her hips slightly, rubbing against his erection and drawing a groan from him. A moment later, he thrust inside her. She gasped at the sudden waves of passion slamming into her. Magick wrapped around them in a lover's embrace, intensifying the pleasure between them. Then she felt it, the threads that would bind them, weaving together to create a beautiful canopy of their future.

He increased his tempo, and each movement pushed them further into ecstasy until he roared in his own release. Ava's body jerked and fell over the edge with him.

Finn rolled to his side and gathered her in his arms. They were silent for a few moments, and she was okay with that. It wasn't awkward; they were just enjoying the bliss, the afterglow. She could feel him in her mind and heart. Her own magick was amped by his, and she wondered if it was the same for him.

"I feel you inside me," he whispered in her ear. "Our souls are connected."

Yes, she knew that. The great thing about it all, she wasn't afraid or regretful. "Together we'll make everything right again." She stretched up and kissed his lips softly. "I'll stay and be your Queen as long as it takes for us to grow annoyed with each other and one of us has to kill the other."

A laugh burst from him. "You have a strange sense of humor."

"I like to keep things interesting."

He flipped her on her back and entered her, filling her once more. Desire rose back up, ready for round two. And so was she.

CHAPTER 8

Since the announcement about the Royal wedding in three days, Ava was ordered by Finn and Kellam not to leave the palace. Both of them feared Quinn would be waiting for her to be alone. Although annoyed, she understood. But still. "I know you said announcing our engagement would protect me from harm, but wouldn't it make Quinn react? I could lure him into a trap."

"No. I can't allow you to be bait. We'll find another way." Finn didn't even look up from the stack of papers he sifted through.

Ava set her jaw. "How long are we going to wait for him to get stupid?"

A chuckle escaped Kellam, the sound surprising her. Up until that moment, the guard had been only serious and grumpy. "Quinn is already stupid."

Laughing, Ava sat back on the sofa and propped her bare feet on the coffee table. "It makes me anxious, knowing he is plotting our deaths and we're just sitting here."

Finn set his pen on his desk and stood. A moment later, he sat beside her and drew her into his lap. "The thought of your life in danger kills me. I am very patient. However, if Quinn touches you, no one will be able to stop my wrath. I beat him once before, and I can do it again."

"Is it because the magick is muted?"

Cocking his head to the side, he narrowed his emerald eyes at her. "Muted? The magick is depleted."

She didn't believe that. Since waking that morning, she was full of power and life. Everything around her was alive, and energy flowed through every flower, animal, and the elements. "I don't think so. I can feel the magick everywhere, but it's dull, like greyed out. It's there, but not within your reach."

Hope lit up Finn's face. "You can reach it?"

She frowned and glanced at Kellam briefly. "I'm not sure...maybe. Since we completed the bond last night, I've been able to see this realm more clearly. But I need to go outside to see if I'm right."

"Right about what."

"That your uncle cursed the land to believing the magick is depleted. He could be keeping it for himself. If so, then he's planning something much bigger than any of us could imagine." Ava shivered. The little visual Sana had showed her would be nothing compared to what Quinn could do with all the magick under his control.

Finn worked his jaw for several moments. "Kellam will take you to test your theories. But you will not go outside the walls surrounding the palace."

"I didn't plan on it. The gardens will be enough for me to connect to the natural world." She kissed him quickly on the lips. "I will be careful. Besides, now that we are bound to one another, you can track me anywhere."

Finn growled low. "I don't want to have to."

"Me either." She kissed him again, letting her mouth linger on his a little longer. "We will stop him, together."

Standing, she waited for Kellam to push off the wall behind Finn's desk and escort her to the gardens. She wasn't sure what she'd find, but it was better than sitting around the study doing nothing. Plus, if she could solve the mystery of the vanishing magick, they'd be one step ahead of Quinn.

Ava stepped out into the cool morning air and breathed in the fragrances of the gardens. Roses, lilies, and the slight scent of jasmine filled her senses. The flowers seemed to hum happily, and the air was full of energy that seemed to recharge her. "Was the air always so alive?"

"It used to be before the war."

She glanced at him and frowned. "You don't feel it now?"

His crimson stare met hers. "No."

By the way his brows dipped and merged together, she could tell it bothered him. So she changed the subject. "Yesterday, in the Wastelands, the rebel called you a demon. Why?"

"Demon in this world is an insult. I'm a changeling, meaning I can take many different forms at will. I can also use the abilities of the creature I shift into. It disturbs some people." A wicked grin curved his mouth.

Ava laughed. "I guess it would."

"There is a stream that runs through the back of the gardens and feeds into a pond. It used to be the strongest source of our power." Kellam increased his steps.

Excitement filled her as she fell into step with him. A free-flowing water source could possibly tell her if the magick was lost or just muted.

Kellam stopped a few feet from a three-foot wide stream, flowing into a large pond. Ava knelt down beside it and dipped her fingers into the cool water. Tingles of electrified energy twined around her hand and up her arm.

"I believe more than ever that the magick is muted. Maybe only from those who were in Edra at the time of the curse or spell or whatever Quinn did to make everyone think the war used up the power." Ava stood and faced Kellam, watching the play of emotions in his features.

"He would want us weak while he built his army."

Ava pursed her lips. Something just wasn't adding up. "Why would he wait so long before acting?" Unless he was waiting for her?

A memory flashed in her mind. Jeff had come into the office a few months ago, mumbling about elves and demons. Ava had paid him no attention. They usually kidded around about paranormal creatures making them late. It was their warped sense of humor. Kind of like telling the teacher the hellhounds ate your homework.

"Kellam, is it possible for elves or anyone from here to cross over to the human realm?"

"Not since your parents left. The Calim King closed all portals in both kingdoms."

"What about the Wastelands?"

Kellam frowned, then slowly shook his head. "He might have been able to."

"I think Quinn or one of his minions killed Jeff, my business partner. They must have found a way to the human realm." Ava hugged her waist as tears stung her eyes. "He was looking for me."

"Ava," Finn called from inside the maze of roses.

"I'm here."

When he came into view, she smiled and relaxed a little. His brows were drawn together, and she guessed he'd heard what she had said. Suddenly, his eyes widened a moment before he screamed her name. Confused, Ava took a step forward, only to be grabbed from behind and pulled under the water.

Finn's screams faded to a muffle then silence as she was dragged through the water. Her lungs burned from holding her breath. She struggled to get loose, and managed to break free. Kicking her legs as hard as she could, she swam to the surface. Once her head broke through the water, she gasped for air.

A hand wrapped around her ankle, and she was jerked under again. After kicking free, she swam away. This time, she glanced at her attacker. *Fuck. Sana.* That bitch wasn't going to best her. Reaching out with her senses, Ava called to the magick within the water as well as the creatures. A school of fish swarmed Sana, giving Ava the time she needed to get to land.

When she emerged from the water, she came face-to-face with Quinn. Before she had a chance to run, he waved a hand in front of her eyes. The world started to fade, and dizziness consumed her.

Damn it. She really had to learn that trick.

CHAPTER 9

Finn roared in fury, then jumped into the pond, hoping to catch the portal before it closed. But Ava was gone, as was the portal Sana had used to grab his mate. And he had no clue where they'd taken her. "She's gone. She was safe inside the property walls and they fucking took her. They breached the wards and took her!"

Kellam mirrored his fury, yet remained calm enough to bark orders to the guards rushing toward them. "Leave no stone unturned until you find Quinn and Sana. That includes the Wastelands."

Finn stormed off to the palace. "I'm going with the party that goes to the Wastelands. For that is the only place he could hide."

"My lord—"

Finn cut Kellam off with a sharp glare. "When I find him, I'm killing him. I won't make the same mistake twice. He kidnapped the Morna Queen and plans to destroy both kingdoms for his personal gain."

After throwing the front door open, he marched to his quarters on the second floor. Fury turned his sight red while his heart broke for the female he'd fallen in love with. He pulled out his scrying mirror and placed his right hand over the runes on the right top corner. "Calim Queen, hear my call."

A few moments passed before Willow's face appeared in the mirror. "I can't see her. How did they get her?"

The Queen could see the future, and sometimes the present, but she had never been able to see into the past. "Sana somehow created a portal in my garden pond. You sure you can't see her?"

"Yes. I searched the moment she vanished. I sensed her panic and tried to connect with her." Willow's eyes filled with tears.

"Then she's in the Wastelands. I'm going to get her back."

Willow nodded. "Do take care."

"I will have guards and warriors with me. Quinn and Sana will not get away with stealing my Queen." After a slight raise of one corner of Willow's lips, Finn ended the communication by lifting his hand from the mirror.

"Everything is ready." Kellam entered the room in battle gear, holding Finn's amour.

It was a good thing his personal guard wasn't going to talk him out of going. He knew better. Taking the chainmail armor, he put it on. "Let's go get the Queen back."

With a nod, Kellam turned on his heels and led Finn down the hall to a pair of winged horses. Charles, the dragon-sabretooth tiger hybrid, waited impatiently by the horses. The beast was ready for battle.

Finn smoothed a hand up Charles's snout. "Today is your day, friend."

Charles replied by blowing a puff of air from his nose, smoke rolling out with it. Then he raised his wings, ready to take off with Finn and the guards.

Finn climbed on his winged horse and took to the sky, flying toward the Wastelands.

Ava paced the small windowless room she'd woken up in minutes before. Or was it hours? She hadn't a clue. There was no magick for her to draw on. No elements to call inside her cell. And she didn't have any hairpins to pick the lock on the door.

A squeak sounded from the rear left corner of the room. She whirled around and spotted a small mouse. "How did you get in here?"

Her heart pounded as hope for an escape rose up within her. Carefully, she crept closer to the mouse. Its ears perked up as it looked directly at her. When she got within a foot from it, the creature scurried up the wall and disappeared behind one of the stones. When Ava touched the wall, she felt an almost silent pulse of magick.

Ha. There you are. She knew there had to be some way out of there. Nothing is ever that airtight or sealed up completely. Sliding her fingers around the stone, she found a crack large enough to fit two fingers inside. Determination to get out of there fueled her strength. She fixated on what little energy was coming through the crack as she pulled on the stone.

After a moment, it moved a fraction of an inch. Excitement sparked in her gut and she doubled her efforts to pull the stone free. But it was short-lived when Sana's voice sounded in Ava's mind. "*What are you up to, little sister?*"

Fucking bitch. "Why don't you come in here and find out?"

Whether it was by magick or being pissed off at her evil half-sister, it was enough to raise her natural power up, breaking whatever had held it at bay. *Good one, Mom. You bound my powers?* And Finn had thought it was from her being raised in the human world. She should have known it was more than that.

With one last jerk, Ava tugged the stone from the wall. To her satisfaction, it was an external wall. The gloom and doom of the Wastelands welcomed her from the small hole. Closing her eyes, she focused on Finn, visualizing his face in her mind. "My King, my love. Do you hear me?"

Nothing happened, and she sagged against the wall. She would not give up. She and Finn would stop Quinn and Sana, but they needed to be connected to do so. Separate, they were weak compared to the evil couple.

"*Ava.*"

Her heart jumped to her throat. "*Finn!*"

"*Thank the gods. I feel you, and Charles has your scent. We're on our way.*"

The door opened, and Ave glared at Sana as she entered with a smirk on her face. "You can try to escape, but you won't get far. You see, by getting into my head like you did yesterday, you linked us together. I can find you anywhere."

Not if I kill you. "Is that supposed to threaten me in some way?"

Sana narrowed her eyes and pursed her lips. "Did you think by bonding with the Morna King you would be strong enough to fight me?"

Ava had to figure out a way to keep the female out of her head. "What do you want besides world destruction and to be Queen Bitch?"

Sana waved away Ava's words, but it appeared to bother her more than she wanted to admit. Good. That told Ava she was getting to her. "Now, name-calling isn't any way to talk to your sister."

Why was she stalling? Ava glanced to the open door behind Sana, causing the female to move into her line of sight. Hmm. She was definitely up to something. "Cut the shit, Sana."

"You are as strong-willed as your parents." Sana stepped closer while Ava's heart skipped several beats. A sad yet satisfying laugh filled the room as Sana continued. "Your father didn't die of old age. One, he wasn't human and couldn't grow old. I do have to give him some points for protecting you, though. The stubborn bastard never plead for his life while I cut off the blood flow to his heart."

Ava fisted her hands at her sides while tears filled her eyes and a lump lodged in her throat. "You're lying."

Sana tsked. "You know I'm not. As for your mother, or *our* mother, she killed herself before I could rip her mind open to find you." Sana's eyes flashed black for a moment, and she rushed toward Ava, gripping her by the throat and pinning her to the wall. "You should be thankful they loved you so much they hid your destiny from you. Thank them for allowing you to grow up weak, like a human."

Fury mounted, igniting the flame deep in Ava's soul. Heat spread throughout her body like it had the day she'd burned Quinn. She welcomed it and willed it to grow. Kenia's words entered her thoughts.

"You may depend on the sun and moon for your magick, but your power also comes from your heart, your emotions. Your passion. You can do anything you desire."

Sana said she'd stopped Ava's father's heart by cutting off the blood flow. Ava wondered if she could do the same. Ava gripped the wrist of Sana's hand that was wrapped around her throat. Sana's pulse beat strong under her fingers, so she focused on slowing it down.

After a few moments, it did, and Sana jerked away, releasing her hold on Ava. Taking advantage of her sister's distraction, Ava thrust a fireball at her. Sana dodged it. The ball hit the wall in the hallway and exploded into a fiery blanket, coating the walls and floors.

Not waiting for the female to react, Ava charged her. She hit Sana in the stomach and knocked her to the ground. Wrapping her fingers around her neck, Ava squeezed and said, "I wish you would lose all your power and ability to use magick. For my parents and all those you ever hurt, that is the least you deserve."

The words just tumbled from her lips without her thinking about what she was really saying. She was so angry, the only punishment short of death she could think of was for Sana to live as a mortal. No magick. Nothing but a shell in a magickal world.

The onyx Kenia had given her, which Ava had hung around her neck earlier that morning, vibrated against her skin. Ava instantly wrapped her free hand around it. Sana saw it, and her eyes grew round. In between gasps of air, Sana said, "You don't know what you just did."

Huh? A moment later, Sana's magickal signature dulled, then faded into nothing. Ava released her and stood. Did she just take her sister's powers from her?

Just then, shouts echoed from down the hallway. Ava turned to the door, only to take a step back. The flames were twice their original size and spreading fast. *Okay, think.* Finn had said she was elemental. Glancing back inside the room, she caught a glimpse of the hole in the wall. Wind. No, that would only fuel the fire.

She needed water. Yet, Kenia had said Ava could do anything she desired. Hesitantly, she reached into the flames and was surprised that they didn't burn her. "I will the fire to stop."

Slowly, the flames lowered until they faded completely. *Wow.*

"Ava!"

She glanced up at Finn's voice and tears filled her eyes. "Finn." She ran to him and threw her arms around him. "Where's Quinn?"

His guards stalked down the hall from different directions, each one shaking their heads. As if the mention of his name had summoned him, Quinn appeared at the end of the hallway. With an evil snear and a growl, he threw an energy bolt at them.

On instinct, Ava threw up her hand, raising a circle, blocking them from Quinn. When the bolt hit the shield, it bounced back and slammed into Quinn's chest. The male fell to the ground, unmoving.

Once Ava took down the circle, Kellam glanced into the room. "What are we to do with her?"

"She's no threat anymore. I took her powers from her. Although, I'm not sure just how I did it. I say send her to Kenia so she can learn to be nice and to live without magick. Like all the people of Edra have had to do for so long." Ava glanced at Finn and then drew her brows together. "If that is what you want to do. You are King, after all."

Finn snaked his arms around her waist and tugged her to him so their bodies meshed together. Desire heated her insides, and she ached to get him alone. One dark brow rose and he smiled as if knowing where her thoughts had gone. "And you are Queen. Your word is law, as well."

"Well, then we need to consult with Willow too since Sana is also a Calim."

Finn nodded. "We can. For now, Sana will go to your great-aunt. If Willow wishes, and thinks death is more suitable, I'll honor her word."

Ava frowned. She wasn't sure she could ever order anyone to death. Well, except for Quinn. He deserved what he got, even though it was self-defense.

"Hey." Finn cupped her chin and turned her face to his. "You restored the magick."

"What? How?"

With a gentle tug, Finn steered her down the hall. "You were right about Quinn cursing Edra and blocking the magick. I'm not sure how he did it, but the moment he died, I felt the snap of the curse breaking. I can feel the magick around us, and I know it's only stronger at home."

A smile formed on her mouth and her heart swelled. The elves of Edra had their lives back. The war was finally over, and the aftermath was no more. She was free to go home.

Home? She was home. These were her people, her family. She belonged in Edra.

Coming to a stop, she framed Finn's face. "I'm falling in love with you. I'm not sure I'll make a good Queen, but I'm willing to try."

His face brightened with happiness. "I fell in love with you the moment I saw you." He kissed her and scooped her up in his arms. A moment later, they materialized in his bedroom at the palace.

"Welcome home, my Queen."

The End

Stay up to date with Lia's news by signing up for her newsletter
http://bit.ly/LiaDavisNewsletter

Thank you so much for taking the time to read my **Skeleton Key** novella!

All reviews are appreciated.

If you would like to read more from the *Skeleton Key* series, please click on the link below:

http://skeletonkeybookseries.com/

About the Author

In 2008, Lia Davis ventured into the world of writing and publishing and never looked back. She has published more than twenty books, including the bestselling *A Tiger's Claim*, book one in her fan favorite Ashwood Falls series. Her novels feature compassionate yet strong alpha heroes who know how to please their women and her leading ladies are each strong in their own way. No matter what obstacle she throws at them, they come out better in the end.

While writing was initially a way escape from real world drama, Lia now makes her living creating worlds filled with magic, mystery, romance, and adventure so that *others* can leave real life behind for a few hours at a time.

Lia's favorite things are spending time with family, traveling, reading, writing, chocolate, coffee, nature and hanging out with her kitties. She and her family live in Northeast Florida battling hurricanes and very humid summers, but it's her home and she loves it!

Follow Lia on Social media:

Website: **http://www.authorliadavis.com/**
Newsletter: **http://bit.ly/LiaDavisNewsletter**

Facebook author fan page:
https://www.facebook.com/pages/Author-Lia-Davis/137761469629592
Facebook Fan Club:
https://www.facebook.com/groups/36882050992 0377/
Twitter: **https://twitter.com/novelsbylia**

Other Books by Lia Davis

Paranormals

Ashwood Falls Series

Winter Eve
A Tiger's Claim
A Mating Dance
Surrendering to the Alpha
A Rebel's Heart
Divided Loyalties
Touch of Desire
A Leopard's Path
Jaguar's Judgment

Birchwood Pack

An Alpha's Fate

Bears of Blackrock
Bear Essentials
Bear Magick
A Beary Sweet Holiday

Sons of War Series

War's Passion
Ashes of War
Artemis's Hunt
Chaotic War
Sons of War Box Set: Volume One

Shifting Magick Trilogy
Moon Curse
Moon Kissed
Moon Mated
Shifting Magick Trilogy box set

Blood and Stone (Vampire Lords)

It's A Vampire Christmas

Contemporaries

Pleasures of the Heart Series

Business Pleasures

Single Titles

His Guarded Heart